BIGMAMA'S
Donald Crews

SCHOLASTIC INC.

New York   Toronto   London   Auckland   Sydney
Mexico City   New Delhi   Hong Kong

For BIGMAMA,
Cottondale and
everybody there—
now and then

Watercolor and gouache
paints were used for the
full-color art. The text type
is Futura Heavy.

ISBN 0-590-22121-3

12 11 10
          1 2/0

Printed in the U.S.A.

"**D**id you see her? Did you see Bigmama?"

We called our Grandma Bigmama. Not that she was big, but she was Mama's Mama.

Every summer we went to see her—Mama, my sisters, my brother, and me. Daddy had to work. He'd come later. It took three days and two nights on the train. Now we were nearly there.

"Cottondale. Cottondale. Next station stop, Cottondale," yelled the conductor to the nearly empty train. "Don't leave no babies on this train." He made the same joke year after year.

SOUTHERN

My uncle Slank came for us by car. We always hoped he'd come with the horse and wagon, but he never did.

We crossed back
over the train tracks,
a turn or two along
the red dirt road, and

onto the lane in front
of Bigmama's house.

Bigmama and Bigpapa
were waiting for us on
the porch. There were
hugs and kisses and
"Oh my, how you've
grown!" and "How
tall you are...is this you?"

Then off with our shoes and socks. We wouldn't need them much in the next few weeks.

Now to see that nothing had changed. In the hall, the sewing machine that you had to pedal like a bicycle. The big clock over the fireplace. The wind-up record player.

The kerosene lamps
and the Sears Roebuck
catalogs. Our room—my brother's
and mine and Uncle Slank's.
Across the hall, the room
where my sisters and
Mama slept. Next to it,
Bigmama's and Bigpapa's room.

Then to the back porch.

Off the porch were three rooms. The tiny extra room no bigger than the bed in it. None of us wanted to sleep there alone. The dining room with the big round table and chairs. And next to it, the kitchen. On the porch was the washstand, where we washed our hands, faces—and feet. At the end of the porch was the well. "Don't fall in," we were told every year. No one ever did!

We stood on tiptoe to
watch the bucket go
down and fill with
water so that we
could have a drink
from the dipper that
hung nearby.

Everything was just
the same.

In the backyard
was the chicken coop,
where Sunday
dinner's chicken spent
its last days.

Behind the shed full of old stuff was the outhouse. Okay now, but scary in the dark.

We stopped for a drink at the pump.

We ran past the pear tree, where the turkeys roosted at night.

Under the tractor in front of the toolshed was a good place to look for nests with eggs in them.

Next to the toolshed was the huge, empty pot for making syrup from sugar cane juice. I dug some worms from the big pile of cane pulp. Wigglers were the best kind for fishing. I chose a pole.

The barn was
another place
to look for eggs.

On to the stable
to see Nancy
and Maude.
Maude was friendly,
but Nancy was a biter.

Down the path, past
the cow pen and the
pig pen, to the pond.
The flat-bottomed
boat was still there.
Plenty of water for
fishing and swimming
this year. Everything
just as it should be.

"A FISH! A FISH!
I GOT ONE,
I GOT ONE!"
I yelled.

"W H O O... W H O O..."
The train whistle.
Dinnertime.

Everybody sitting around the table that filled the room— Bigmama, Bigpapa, Uncle Slank, our cousins from down the road, and all of us. We talked about what we did last year. We talked about what we were going to do this year. We talked so much we hardly had time to eat.

The night was jet
black except for
millions of stars.
We could hardly
sleep thinking about
things to come.